KUSA'S BIG SURPRISE!

Written by
Kathy Iorio

Illustrated by
Chris Schroeder

Foreword

With a message of self-love, self-respect and selflessness, Kusa's Big Surprise! is a wonderful story and powerful reminder for readers of all ages. Kathy Iorio masterfully takes readers on a special journey as Kusa discovers her very own gift of a lifetime.

Through vibrant imagery and relatable characters, readers of all generations will love the reassuring message and life lessons Kusa learns along the way. Discover for yourself the timeless message of Kusa's Big Surprise! as you share this story with those around you, especially children.

Caregivers and educators will appreciate the relevant talking points Kathy provides as they allow for a genuine and personal conversation about the story in such a way that reinforces the beauty and full potential within each of us to love others as we fully love ourselves.

Dr. Matthew J. Patterson
Assistant Superintendent of Elementary Education
West Jefferson Hills School District

Dedication

To all children who need encouragement to be
themselves and to treat others
with respect and kindness, and in
loving memory of my dear mother, Betty Morgan.

Acknowledgments

I am grateful to my husband and best friend, Tony Snow, M.D., for his unwavering and loving support; to my dad, Randy Owens, for his belief in me; to my godmother, Barbara O'Brien, for her caring support throughout my childhood; and to God, who provided the inspiration to write this book.

A special thanks to Amy Luce, educator and writer, for her exceptional editing support. Thank you to Marsha Blessing and the team at Orison Publishers, Inc. for coaching and assisting me in this publishing adventure. Their input and excellent publishing expertise was invaluable and deeply appreciated.

Testimonials

Kusa's Big Surprise! is a positive story which encourages children not only to be kind and helpful to others, but also to have self-confidence in their daily lives. The author emphasizes that simple acts of kindness are important in each child's personal development. The storyline is refreshing and definitely teaches a lesson that all of us, no matter what age, can benefit from by reading this delightful book! As a former elementary school teacher for decades, I find the lessons taught in this book to be invaluable and very relevant, especially in today's world. I highly recommend this book!

Patricia Visnosky, Teacher

As a busy, working mom of two boys, five and seven, we are always looking for ways to embrace their differences, while reinforcing the importance of being kind, helping others and being YOU. *Kusa's Big Surprise!* is just that book! My children were captivated by Kusa and her journey. The vibrant illustrations along with the talking points at the end make it such a wonderful, engaging and educational experience for our entire family. From start to finish, my children, along with yours, will enjoy searching for the hidden creatures and fall in love with all the animals along the way. *Kusa's Big Surprise!* is definitely a book you will want to add to your at-home library. It is relatable and relevant for all ages. It has become a family favorite!

Sarah Hale, R.D., Parent

Kusa was a curious young elephant. She loved to play, explore, roll in the mud and spray her body on hot days.

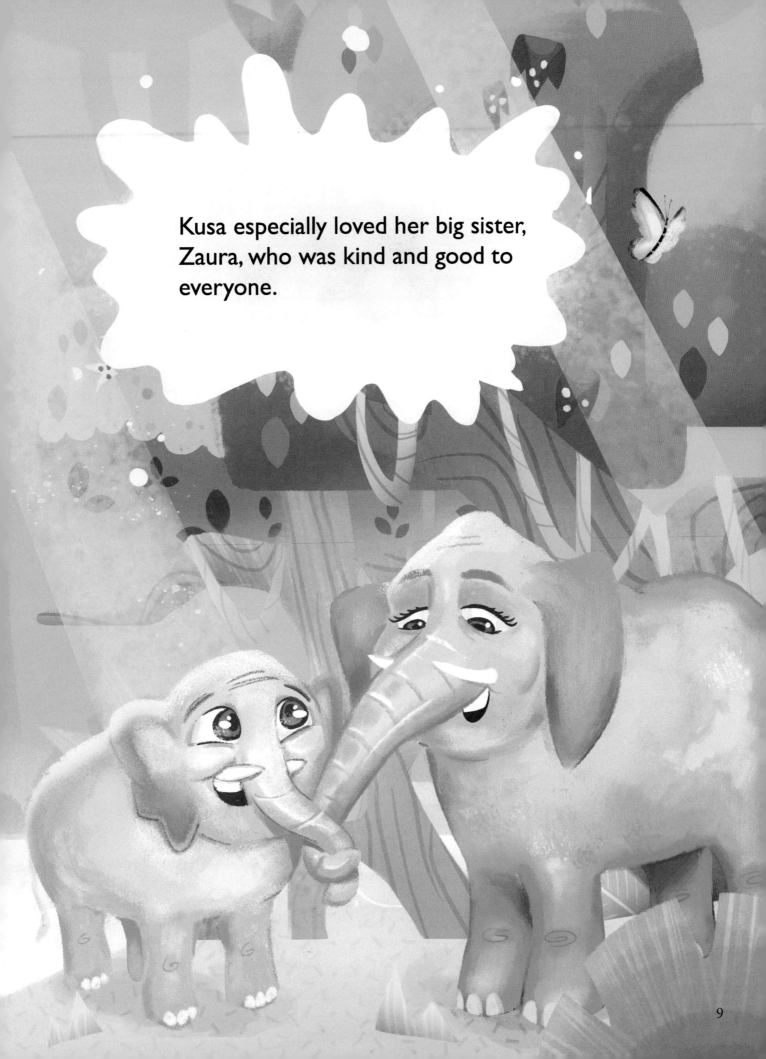

Kusa especially loved her big sister, Zaura, who was kind and good to everyone.

Kusa wanted to be just like her sister, and so she set out to find someone to help. It didn't take long. As she passed the mud hole, she saw a baby elephant stuck in the muck. He was starting to cry. Kusa knew just how to get out, and she showed him. Kusa's kind act made the baby elephant happy!

Kusa continued on her way and saw her friend Speedy, the antelope, who looked frightened. "Speedy," said Kusa. "Can I help you?"

Speedy said, "I'm lost and can't find my family."

Kusa patted him with her trunk and said, "I'm tall. Let me see what I can see." Kusa looked around and spotted Speedy's family. "They're right over that hill!" She smiled as Speedy ran to join them.

"Thanks, Kusa!" Speedy called as he sped off.

As she continued walking, Kusa heard a familiar chirp, chirp song, but it was a sad chirp. "Buddy?" said Kusa. She looked around and then up. There was Buddy, perched in a tree, looking unhappy.

"What's wrong?" Kusa asked.

"I'm sad because my friends are off having fun without me," he said.

"Well, I'm your friend, too, Buddy! Let's play together!" Kusa said.

Buddy started singing, "Chirp, chirp, chirp, chirp, chirp!" They played until it was time for Buddy to go home. "Thanks, Kusa!" Buddy said. "You cheered me up!"

Kusa was happy. "Another kind deed, just like Zaura would do!"

Feeling thirsty after her busy day, Kusa went to the watering hole. While she drank, she saw her reflection and noticed that something was wrong. How could she not have seen this before?

Her ears were small, not big and floppy like Zaura's!

Shocked, Kusa started for home to tell Mom and Dad. She had not gone far when she heard Buddy singing, "Chirp, chirp, chirp, chirp, chirp!" Kusa cried out, "Buddy, I just realized my ears are small, not big and floppy like Zaura's!"

"Kusa, the size of your ears doesn't matter!" he said. "I like you just the way you are!"

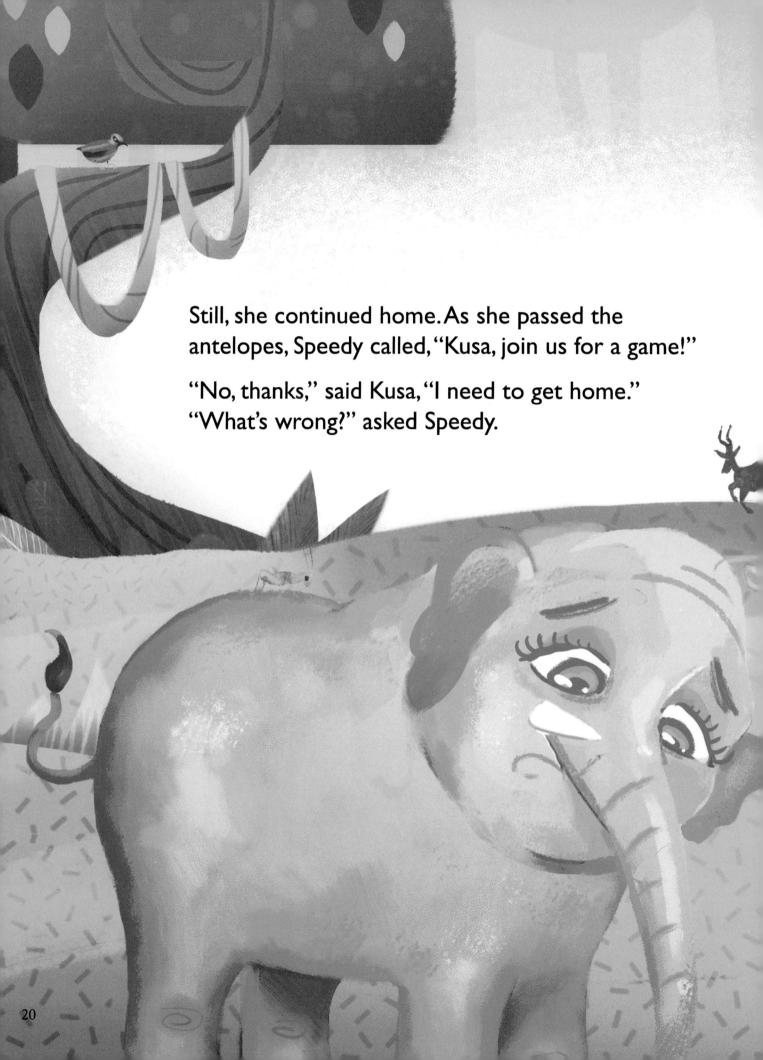

Still, she continued home. As she passed the antelopes, Speedy called, "Kusa, join us for a game!"

"No, thanks," said Kusa, "I need to get home." "What's wrong?" asked Speedy.

20

"I just realized my ears are small and different!" Kusa said.

"Kusa," said Speedy, "we all come in different shapes and sizes."

Kusa nodded but continued walking.

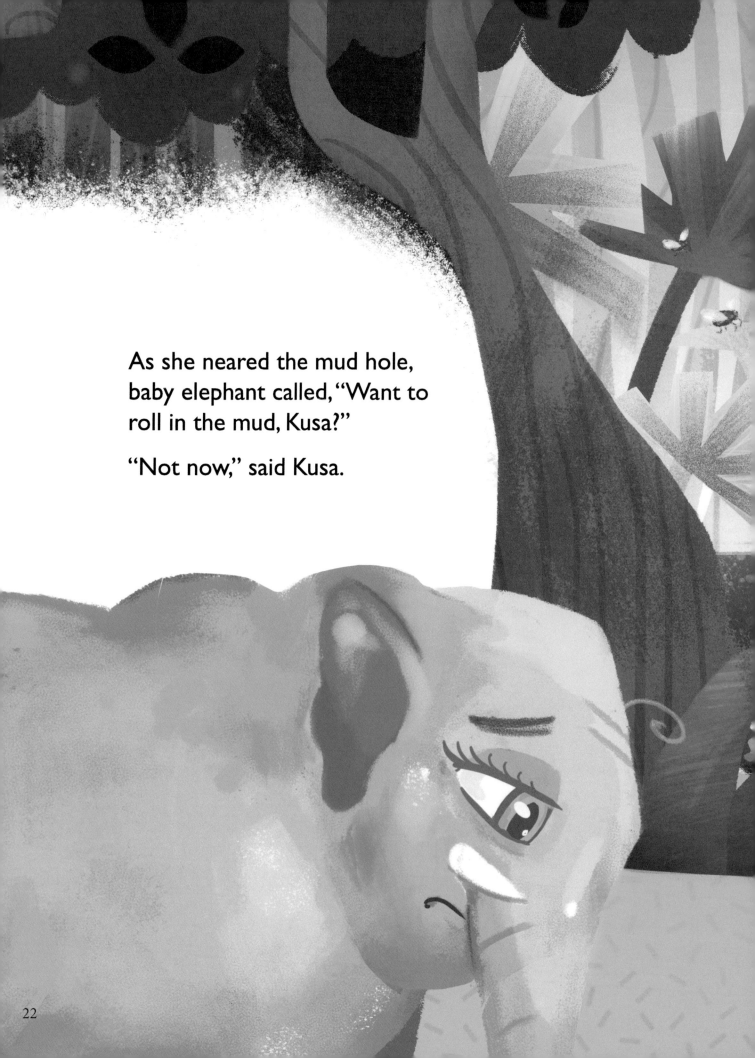

As she neared the mud hole, baby elephant called, "Want to roll in the mud, Kusa?"

"Not now," said Kusa.

"I'm too upset to play because my ears look different from other elephants' ears!"
"But Kusa," said baby elephant, "kind people are amazing no matter what they look like."

Still, Kusa trudged on. When she finally got home, Mom and Dad greeted her.

Kusa burst into tears. "I want to be just like Zaura. So, I tried to do good deeds all day!" "And did you?" asked Mom. "Well, yes," said Kusa, "but I also saw something I never noticed before!"

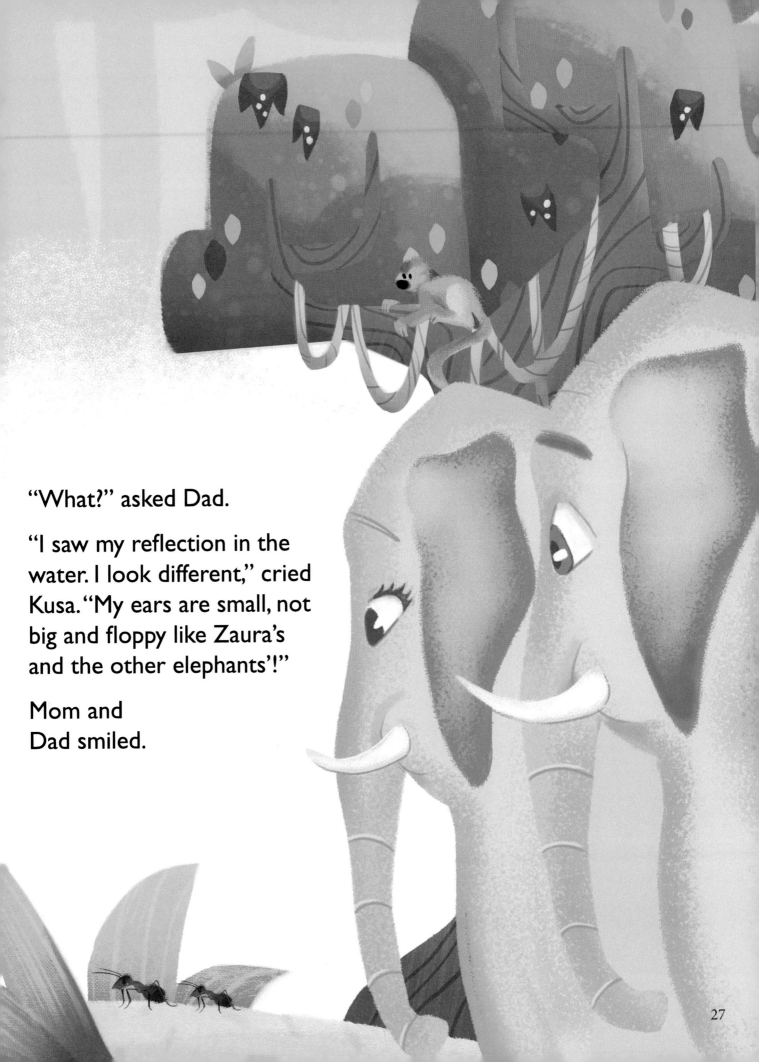

"What?" asked Dad.

"I saw my reflection in the water. I look different," cried Kusa. "My ears are small, not big and floppy like Zaura's and the other elephants'!"

Mom and Dad smiled.

Dad said, "Kusa, do you think we love you because of your tusks, feet, body or ears?"

"No, I guess not," Kusa said.

"Well, why do we love you?" mom asked.

Kusa thought. "You love me because I'm me?"

"Yes!" said Mom and Dad.

"And I bet your friends would say the same!"

Kusa thought about this and about her day. "Well, Buddy said he likes me just the way I am. Baby elephant said that when you are kind, you are amazing—no matter what you look like. And Speedy said we all come in different shapes and sizes."

"Your friends are right!" Mom said, "I know someone who would love to hear all about what you learned today!"

"Who?" asked Kusa, looking around.

"Me!" said Zaura as she came out from behind some trees. "Zaura!" cried Kusa. "I so want to be just like you!"

"But Kusa, that's silly," Zaura replied, "because you make such an amazing, one-of-a-kind you!"

That made Kusa very happy.

The next time Kusa saw her reflection, she looked at her ears and smiled. She really was an amazing, one-of-a-kind elephant. She loved being herself and being kind to others, too.

So, be a one-of-a-kind, amazing YOU and be kind to others, too!

Let's Talk

Kusa learns it's important to be yourself.

1. What do you think it means to be yourself?

2. Why do you think people come in so many different shapes, sizes and abilities?

3. What would it be like if we were all exactly the same?

4. When you look at your reflection in the mirror, what is something positive you can say about yourself?

5. Do a group activity where your family members and/or classmates each take a turn saying one positive thing they like about each person.

Kusa learns how important it is to be kind.

1. Think of a time when you were kind to someone. What did you do that was kind? How did it make you feel?

2. How do you think it makes other people feel when you are kind to them?

3. What are some ways you can be kind to your family? Your friends? Yourself?

4. What kind things can you do when someone is feeling sad?

5. Why is it important to be kind to others?

ELEPHANT FUN FACTS

- Being part of a family is important for elephants, and so they travel in groups called herds. An elephant herd can range from 8 to 100 elephants.

- Elephants spend 16 hours a day eating lots of fruit, grasses, bananas, tree bark and more. It takes a lot of eating to fuel such a powerful animal!

- Elephants can hear through their feet by sending sound waves in the ground. They can communicate with other elephants as far as 5 miles away. Just amazing!

- Elephants can swim and use their trunk to breathe when they are under water. It's like they are snorkeling!

- We have over 600 muscles in our bodies. However, elephants have over 40,000 muscles just in their trunk!

- Elephants have emotions. They can cry, play, laugh and they have great memories, too.

- Elephants are happy when they are moving their tails side to side swatting flies.

- Elephants use their trunks to hug and show they care.

- Elephants can see themselves in a mirror.

- Elephant tusks are actually teeth.

BE A CRITTER CATCHER!

Find, identify and count the hidden critters on each page.

Butterfly **Ant** **Fly** **Worm** **Dragon fly**

Frog **Bird** **Monkey** **Grasshopper**

Answer Key: Pg 8-9 Dragonfly, Butterfly, Grasshopper Pg.10-11 Fly, Worm, Frog, Ant Pg. 12-13 Dragonfly, Grasshopper, Ant Pg. 14-15 Dragonfly, Ant, Grasshopper Pg. 16-17 Frog, Grasshopper, Fly Pg. 18-19 Frog, Dragonfly, Ant Pg. 20-21 Bird, Grasshopper, Worm Pg. 22-23 Two flies, Bird, Worm Pg. 24-25 Two Grasshoppers, dragonfly Pg. 26-27 Monkey, Grasshopper, Two Ants Pg. 28-29 Dragonfly, Worm, Frog Pg. 30-31 Bird, Fly, Grasshopper Pg.32-33 Bird, Grasshopper, Ant

Made in the USA
Middletown, DE
15 May 2021